This book belongs to:

For Kate and Anna
E. B.

For Louise,
from Greg!

This edition published by Scholastic Inc.,
557 Broadway; New York, NY 10012,
by arrangement with Little Tiger Press.
SCHOLASTIC and associated logos are trademarks
and/or registered trademarks of Scholastic Inc.
Scholastic Canada; Markham, Ontario

ISBN-10: 1-84506-443-7 • ISBN-13: 978-1-84506-443-3

Text copyright © Elizabeth Baguley 2005
Illustrations copyright © Magi Publications 2005

Original edition published in English by Little Tiger Press,
an imprint of Magi Publications, London, England, 2005.

This edition copyright © Good Books, Intercourse, PA 17534, 2005

Printed in China.

MEGGIE MOON

ELIZABETH BAGULEY

illustrated by
GREGOIRE MABIRE

Digger and Tiger spent all their time in the Yard. Nothing grew there but piles of dented things, empty things, worn-out things. No one else dared come to the Yard. It was *their* place.

Digger and Tiger were
rough-and-tumble boys,
spiky-haired, hole-at-the-knee boys.
They were not brothers, but they went
together like a garbage can and its lid.

One day a girl arrived. She walked through the high gate and clicked it shut behind her. She stared at the tangled rubble and the king-of-the-castle boys. The boys stared back.

"I'm Meggie Moon," said the girl. "Can I play with you?"

"We don't play with girls," snarled Tiger.

"Girls don't know how to play," hissed Digger.

"Oh, don't they?" said Meggie, laughing.

Meggie left the boys standing in the shadows and went to explore. The Yard was a mess and the boys were unfriendly, but Meggie had ideas.

She picked up some of the
trash and began
to arrange it . . .

a tin here and
a pipe there . . .

until . . .

"It's a racing car!" said Tiger.
"You can drive it if you want," offered Meggie.
"Not likely," said Digger.

But as soon as Meggie left,
the boys jumped into the car
and raced away until dark.

The next day Meggie
came to the Yard again.
Digger and Tiger watched
her picking over the junk.
  "Come on, build something!"
ordered Tiger.
  So Meggie made a ship.
When it was finished,
the boys played pirates.
  "Can I come aboard?"
she asked.
  "I suppose you
could be our cook,"
said Tiger.

"I'd rather be your lookout," said Meggie.
She spit on her hands, shot up the
rigging and shouted, "Ship in view!"
   Startled, the boys raised their binoculars.
"Aye-aye, shipmate!" they said.

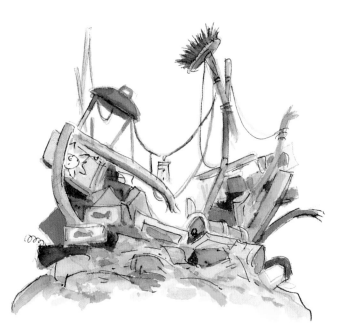

By the third day the car was mangled and the ship wrecked.

"Let's kick cans," said Tiger.

"I'd rather throw stones," whined Digger.

"That's boring," said Meggie. "Why don't we make a den?"

She found wall-things and roof-things and the boys crammed and jammed them into a corner. They played until dark when the bed calls came.

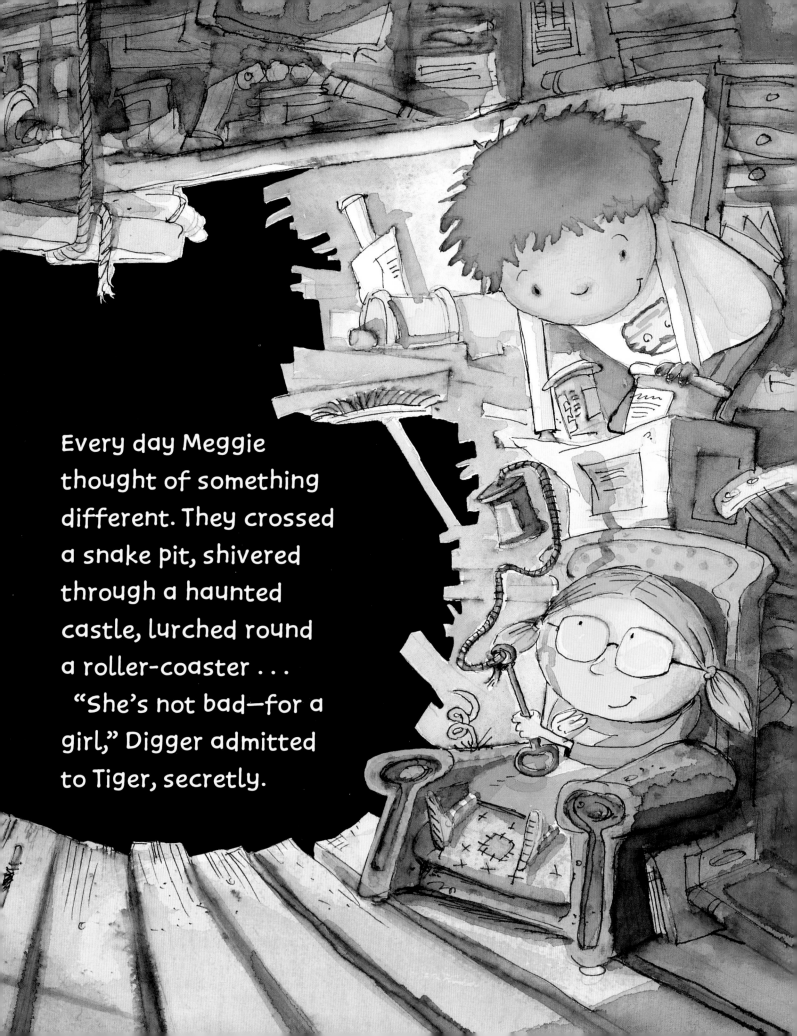

Every day Meggie thought of something different. They crossed a snake pit, shivered through a haunted castle, lurched round a roller-coaster . . .

"She's not bad—for a girl," Digger admitted to Tiger, secretly.

Then, one day, Meggie announced,
"I'm going home tomorrow."
The boys gazed at the Yard.
They remembered how, before Meggie
came, the rubble was just rubble.
"But what will we play?"
wailed Digger.

"I've brought you a good-bye present.
You can play with that."
   Meggie wheeled in a towering
load and toppled it in
front of them.

"Space explorers at the
ready!" she commanded,
then marched out through
the gate, clicking it shut
behind her.

"Aye-aye, Captain," Digger and Tiger saluted, but Meggie had gone. The sound of the closing gate echoed through the Yard.

The boys stared emptily after
Meggie. At last they inched towards
her present-pile. The heap of rubble
was just . . . a porthole here,
a jet there . . .
   The boys looked at each other.
They had ideas.

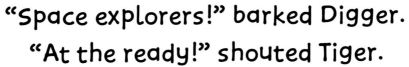

"Space explorers!" barked Digger.
"At the ready!" shouted Tiger.

By dusk, smooth
things and crumpled
things . . .

shattered things and
battered things . . .

spiraled high
above the Yard
fence.

With spacesuits on, the astronauts
climbed into the rocket.

"Blast off!" they chorused. Digger and
Tiger roared and rumbled away from the Yard,
over the city, zooming into space in search of
their lost captain, Meggie, Meggie Moon.